**BOOK TWO
STARABELLA
IN THE
COMMUNITY**

New Adventures and Mixed Emotions

Written by Sharon Fialco

Based on Music Composed and Performed by Tara Fialco

Narrated and Sung by Dana Fialco

Illustrated by Anton Petrov

PLAY THE CD TO HEAR THE STORY AND MUSIC
CAPTIONS ARE INCLUDED IN THE BOOK

OTHER BOOKS IN THE STARABELLA SERIES

STARABELLA
Mystery Girl of Music

STARABELLA
Welcome to a Bright New World

CD RECORDINGS ALSO AVAILABLE

The Three-Book Series Music Soundtrack

The CD Single "A New Beginning"

Published by Fialco Productions, Inc.
205 E. 95th Street, Suite 30K
New York, NY 10128

business@starabella.com

Copyright © and ℗ 2010 by Fialco Productions, Inc.
Art Direction by Sharon Fialco
Book Design by Susanna Yoffe, CG+M Advertising, New York, NY

All rights reserved.
No portion of this book or recording may be reproduced—mechanically, electronically, or by any other means, including, without limitation, photocopying, recording, and digital transfer—without the prior written permission of the publisher and copyright owner, Fialco Productions, Inc.
Printed in China

SUMMARY: When Mommy and Daddy take Starabella out into the community, they are confused by her sometimes unusual reactions and behaviors (such as oversensitivity to light and sound at the circus and disregarding safety rules at acrobatics class); however, recognizing her unique talents and abilities, they realize that the most important thing is for Starabella to BELIEVE IN HERSELF.

Publisher's Cataloging-in-Publication Data
(Prepared by The Donohue Group, Inc.)

Fialco, Sharon.
  Starabella / written by Sharon Fialco ; based on music composed and performed by Tara Fialco ; narrated and sung by Dana Fialco ; illustrated by Anton Petrov.
     v. : col. ill. ; cm. + sound discs. -- (Starabella : bright new world series)

  This collection was inspired by the childhood music and experiences of the author's daughter, Tara. Dealing with autism, Tara composed music to express her thoughts and feelings.
  CD recording produced by Joe Vulpis, AP Music, Inc.
  Each book contains a note at head of title: Bk.1. Starabella at home -- bk.2. Starabella in the community -- bk.3. Starabella at school.
  Each book has an accompanying CD containing the narrated story with music.
  Summary: The story of Starabella, a musically talented little girl with learning differences, full of mystery and surprise.
  Incomplete contents: Bk. 1. Mystery girl of music -- bk. 2. New adventures and mixed emotions -- bk. 3. Welcome to a bright new world
  ISBN: 978-0-9715880-3-5 (set)

1. Autistic children--Juvenile fiction. 2. Mainstreaming in education--Juvenile fiction. 3. Musical ability--Juvenile fiction. 4. Inclusive education--Juvenile fiction. 5. Social interaction in children--Juvenile fiction. 6. Learning disabilities--Juvenile fiction. 7. Autistic children--Fiction. 8. Mainstreaming in education--Fiction. 9. Musical ability--Fiction. 10. Learning disabilities--Fiction. I. Fialco, Tara. II. Fialco, Dana. III. Petrov, Anton, 1977- IV. Vulpis, Joe. V. AP Music Entertainment, Inc. VI. Title.

PZ7.F53 S73 2010
[Fic]

2009906619

Library of Congress Control Number: 2009906619
ISBN: 978-0-9715880-1-1

To order your copy of Book One, Book Two, Book Three, the complete three-book series, the three-book series music soundtrack, or the CD single "A New Beginning," please visit www.starabella.com.

Introduction

Come along with Starabella as she ventures into the community with her parents. She has a wonderful time but runs into difficulty meeting expectations for appropriate behaviors, conformity, and following the rules. This causes her to have a "Mixture of Feelings." Through it all, Starabella expresses her many emotions and thoughts through her music.

Starabella's parents become concerned about their daughter and face confusion about how to react. They come to understand that Starabella must reach for her own personal goals in her own unique way since **NOTHING IS MORE IMPORTANT THAN FOR STARABELLA TO BELIEVE IN HERSELF.**

As listeners/readers root for Starabella, she will inspire them to turn their own **DREAMS INTO REALITY.**

But remember: "Safety first!"

This story was inspired by the childhood music and experiences of the author's daughter Tara. Dealing with autism, Tara composed music to create a magical, musical world of empathy, acceptance of others, and acceptance of self.

Guide to Listening to & Reading This Story

This book contains illustrated pages and a fully narrated CD, complete with page-turn instructions. The illustrations include captions taken from the narration to help listeners follow along. The combined audio and visual presentation of the story enhances comprehension.

When children listen to this story with a caring adult, the CD can be paused at various points to provide opportunities for discussion of feelings and ideas prompted by the story.

Since the story is narrated, children also have the option to listen to the story on their own.

Children can use the illustrations as a guide to retell the story in their own words when not listening to the CD.

PLEASE ENJOY THE STORY AND SING, DANCE, DREAM, AND IMAGINE ALONG WITH THE MUSIC.

Chapter One
The Exciting Circus

"Who wants to go to the circus?" called Daddy.

"Me! Me!" shouted Starabella, jumping for joy.

Starabella, Mommy, and Daddy arrived at the arena.

The darkened room looked like it was filled with multicolored stars. But nothing shined as brightly as Starabella's own eyes.

Bliing!

"Ladies and gentlemen, boys and girls, get ready to be thrilled by the most spectacular, the most amazing, the most dazzling show i-n-n-n our galaxy!"

Through a kaleidoscope of whirling colors and motion, Starabella watched, spellbound.

The Clown
(Instrumental)

Trapeze artists are so brave, thought Starabella. She wished she were one of them. She imagined herself this way:

The Exciting Circus

LYRICS: PAGE 30

Starabella covered her head with her arms. *What's happening?*

The people around her in the audience whispered "Shhh!" and scowled angrily at Starabella, Mommy, and Daddy.

In the car on their way home, Starabella hummed her sad tune.

**Feelings of the Past
(Instrumental)**

Would the Oclaifs ever understand what had happened to Starabella at the circus?

Chapter Two
A Mixture of Feelings

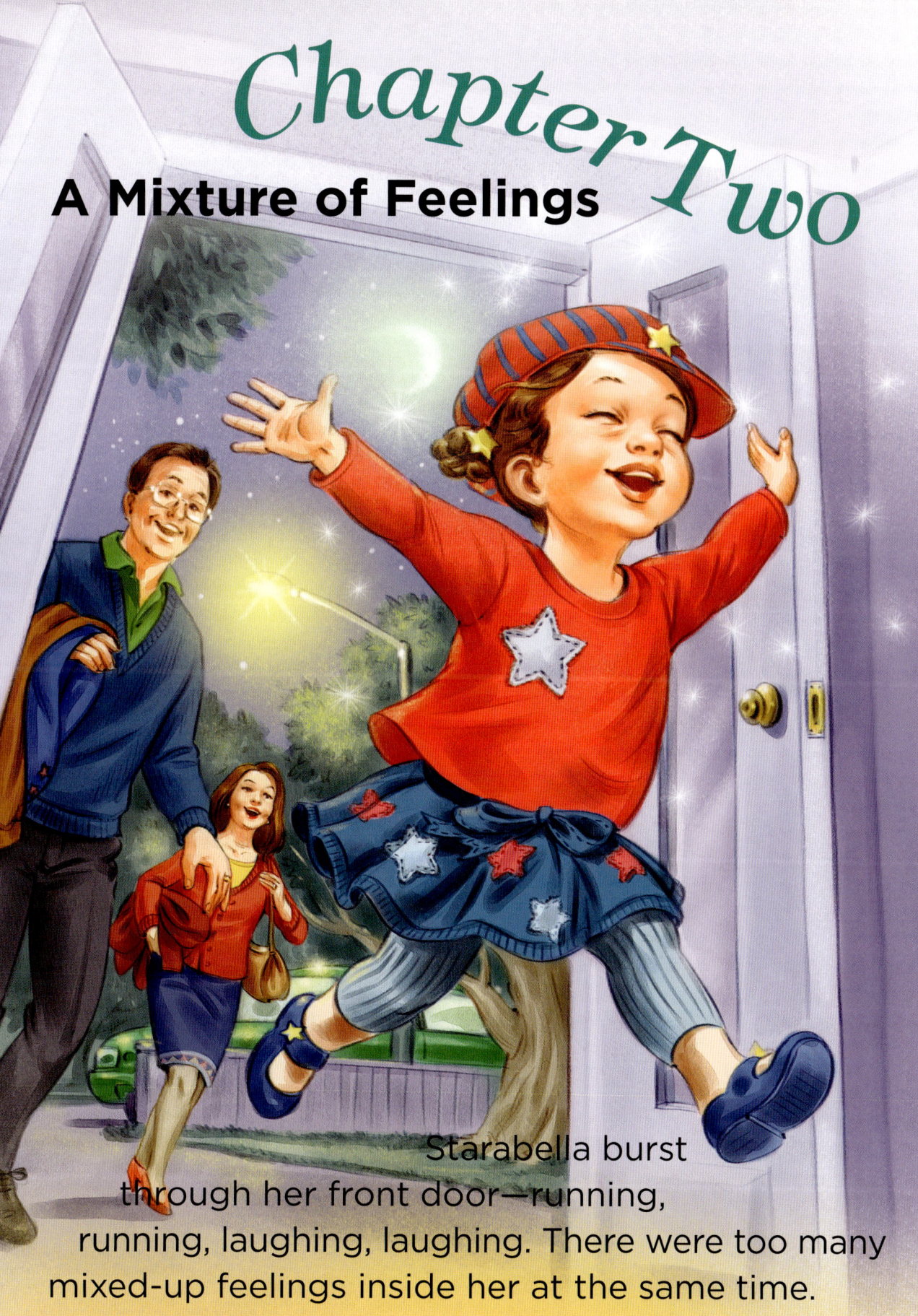

Starabella burst through her front door—running, running, laughing, laughing. There were too many mixed-up feelings inside her at the same time.

Starry sped around the dining room table—ZOOM!
—through the living room—ZOOM!
—up the stairs and back down again—ZOOM!

"Starry, stop!"
Daddy pleaded.

Starabella raced over to her beloved piano and began to pour her feelings into her music.

**A Mixture of Feelings
(Instrumental)**

As each note rang out with Starry's emotions, another emotion, brighter than all the rest, came shining through. It was HOPE.

Bliing!

Mommy chose the brightest star in the sky and made a wish:

"Please, star, watch over Starry. Let the light that's shining through her eyes continue to shine."

The stars in the sky lit up even more brilliantly, then beamed down upon Starry, encircling her in star-glow.

"Look-a-me!" cried Starry.

"What just happened?" asked Mommy.

"It's a mystery," said Daddy.

Chapter Three
Ta-da!

Three times a week, Starry and Mommy attended acrobatic classes for toddlers, called Tumbling Tots, at their neighborhood gym.

***I'm on My Way
(Instrumental)***

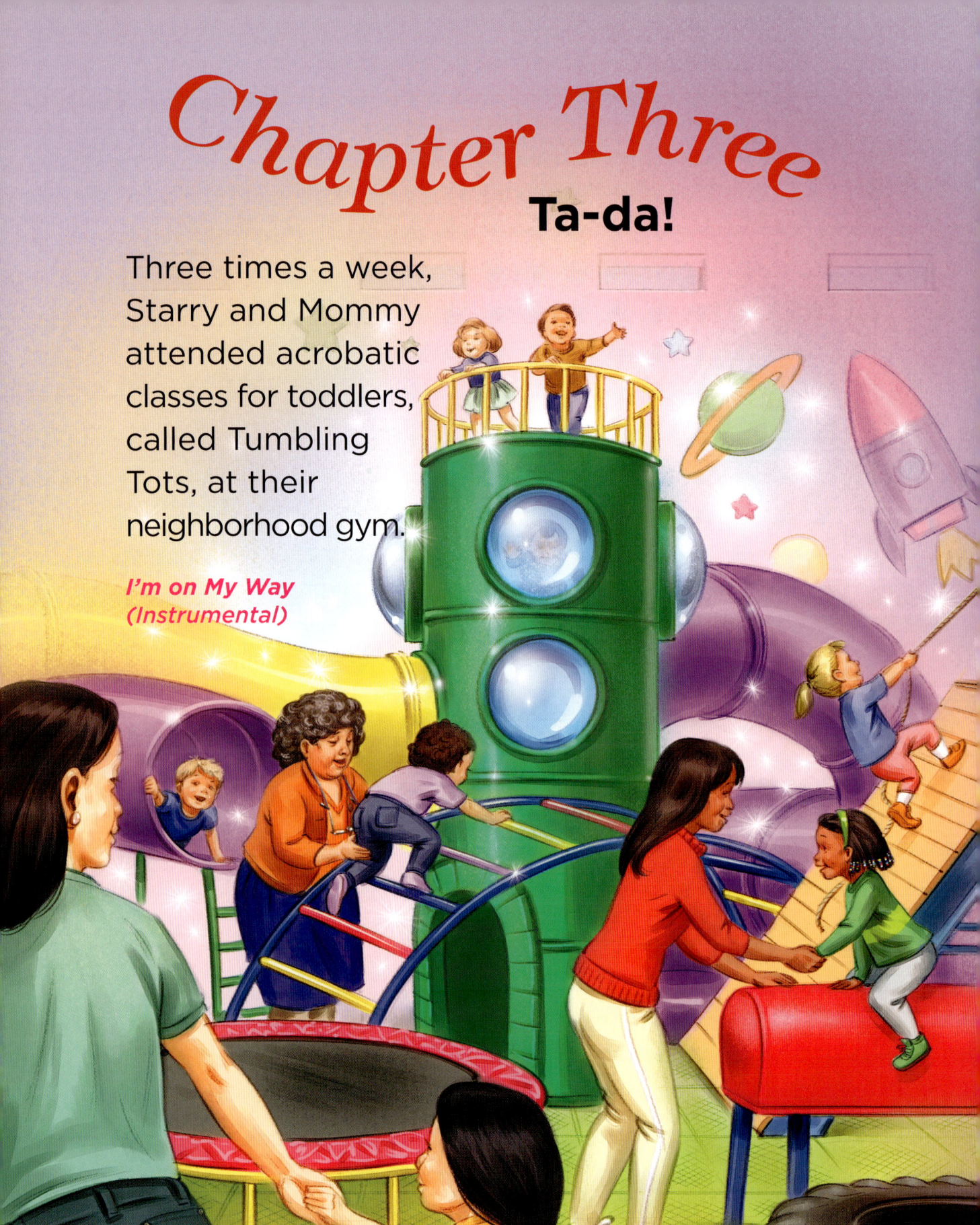

One day, special visitors came to the class—they were firefighters. They came to show the children a tall, two-story ladder that they used to rescue people in danger.

Everybody got to take a turn climbing the ladder.

Starabella was the last to get a turn on the ladder.

"Look at that little girl go!"

All heads turned upward.

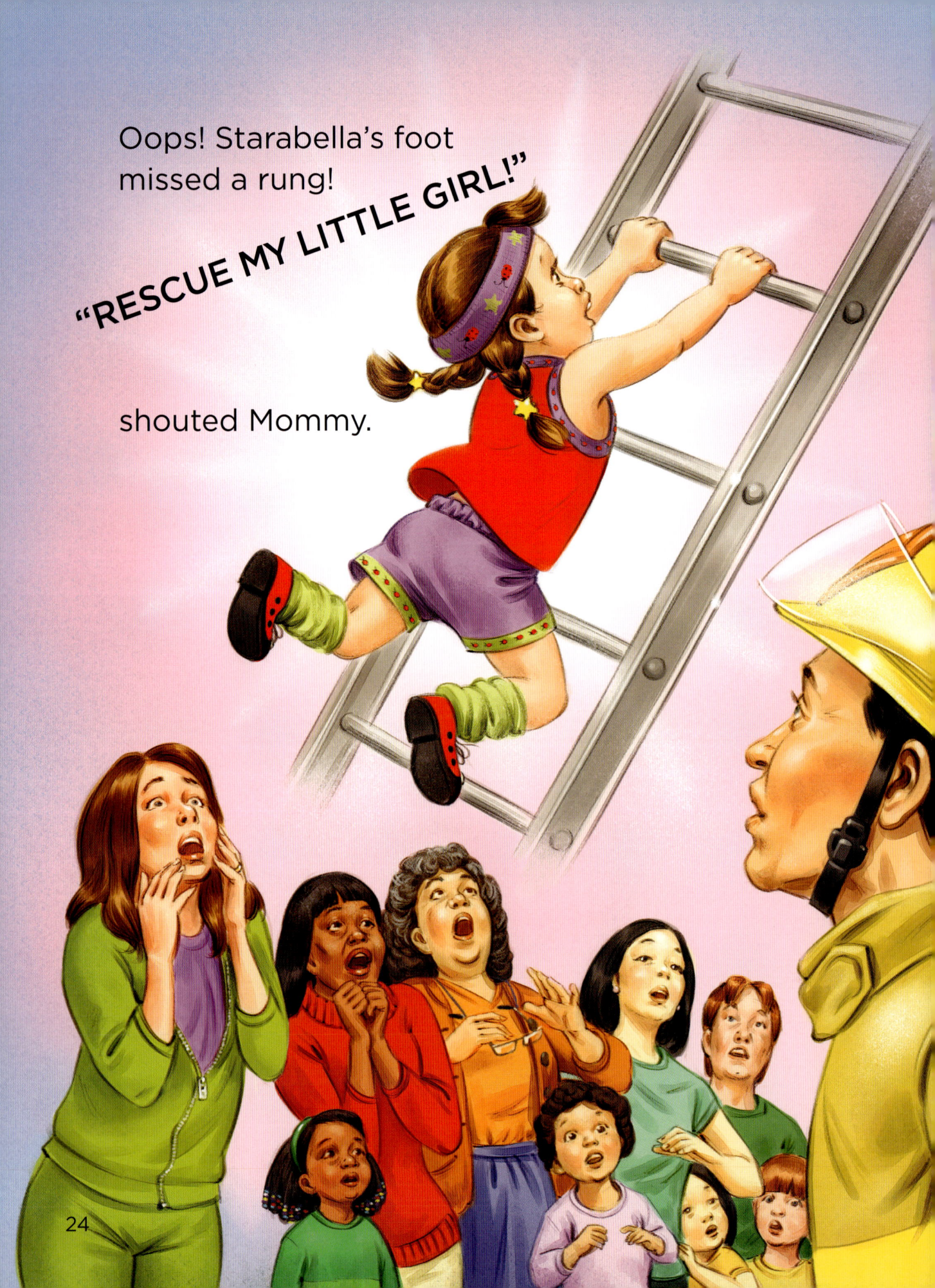

Oops! Starabella's foot missed a rung!

"RESCUE MY LITTLE GIRL!"

shouted Mommy.

"Ta-da!" Starabella shouted. She waved to everyone below.

"Never do anything like that again!" Mommy scolded, wagging her finger in Starry's face.

Mommy reached down (shakily) and hugged Starabella and smothered her with kisses.

Starabella's eyes shined in the brightness of Mommy's lopsided smile.

Bliing!

The stars in the sky winked at Starabella through an opening in her curtain. Starabella's eyes shined right back.

Bliing! Bliing! Bliing! Bliing! Bliing!

As confused as the Oclaif family could sometimes be, Mr. and Mrs. Oclaif were absolutely sure of one thing:

Nothing made them feel prouder than being Starabella's mommy and daddy.

Put your hands up in the air and shout
TA-DA!

THE EXCITING CIRCUS

Starry's in the big top—
  she takes center ring
Twirling and swirling,
  she makes our hearts sing
Climbing the ladder
  to fly without wings
The crowd's cheering—
  they are hearing music sound
As their hearts pound—
  so stick around, she's ready
  to swing!

Starry's on the trapeze—
  up high in midair
(Oooh!)
Swooping and looping,
  she hasn't a care
(Aaah!)
"LOOK AT ME—I'M FLYING!"
  so watch if you dare!
(Oh!)

Swinging and soaring while she's
Floating, flipping, never slipping,
 fingers gripping—
Circus star flair!

La-la, la; la-la, la
La, la, la, la, la, la

Stirring the crowd to a starry-eyed state
Starry is starring in the circus now
She takes a bow—
(Yea!)
She's Starabella the Great!

Ta-da!

TA-DA!

Ta-da
Ta-da

When you're feelin' scared
 inside and don't know why
When you feel like you may
 even want to cry
All you have to do is give it
 your best try
Then throw your hands up
 to the sky and shout, Ta-da!
Ta-da ta-da ta-da! Ta-da!
Ta-da ta-da!

Ta-da ta-da! Ta-da ta-da!
Ta-da ta-da! Ta-da!

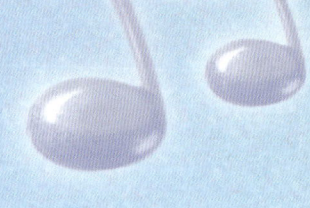

When you want some sunshine
 but get rain instead
When you wish that you could
 go right back to bed
Smile and sing a song about
 the rain instead
Then throw your hands above
 your head and shout, Ta-da!
Ta-da ta-da ta-da! Ta-da!
Ta-da ta-da!

There'll be scary times and
 sad times, too
Just remember what you've
 got to do:
Hold your head up proud
And sing out nice and loud
Watch that crowd be wowed
And shout, Ta-da!
Ta-da ta-da ta-da! Ta-da!
Ta-da ta-da!

[Musical interlude]

Ta-da ta-da! Ta-da ta-da!
Ta-da ta-da! Ta-da!

When you feel that life
  sometimes just isn't fair
When you want to hide away
  but don't know where
Believe in who you are
  and in your special flair
Then throw your hands up
  in the air and shout, Ta-da!
Ta-da ta-da ta-da! Ta-da!
Ta-da ta-da!
Shout, Ta-da! Ta-da ta-da
Shout, Ta-da! Ta-da ta-da
Shout, Ta-da! Ta-da ta-da
Shout, Ta-da!!!!!!

Book Two Recording Credits

PERFORMANCES
(in order of appearance)

Narrator:	Dana Fialco
Daddy:	Matt Castle
Starabella:	Dana Fialco
Mommy:	Dana Fialco
Vendor #1:	Nunzio Vulpis
Vendor #2:	Joe Vulpis
Ringmaster:	Reggie Sinkler
Firefighter #1:	Joe Vulpis
Firefighter #2:	Matt Castle
Firefighter #3:	Larry Romano
Other Mommy:	Ann Vulpis
Worried Whisperers:	Louise McConnell
	Maria de Lalinde
	Ann Vulpis
	Joe Vulpis
Kids' Counting Chorus:	Meghan Dizon
	Stephanie Dizon
	Noah Sidotti
	Ariana Sidotti
	Joe Vulpis

I'm on My Way (0:49)

Concept, Title, and Music Written by: Tara Fialco

Keyboard: Tara Fialco

Vocal Humming: Dana Fialco

Programming: Rich Mercurio

Additional Keyboards/Programming: Joe Vulpis

Acoustic Guitar: Oz Noy

Upright Bass: Bernie Minoso

The Clown (1:12)

Concept, Title, and Music Written by: Tara Fialco

Synthesizer: Tara Fialco

Programming: Rich Mercurio

Additional Keyboards/Synthesizers/Bass: Joe Vulpis

Soprano Saxophone: Daniel Lapidus

The Exciting Circus (1:38)
Concept, Title, and Music Written by: Tara Fialco

Lyrics Written by: Dana Fialco

Additional Lyrics Written by: Sharon Fialco

Piano Keyboard/Fender Rhodes/Organ: Tara Fialco

Vocals: Dana Fialco

Background Vocals: Dana Fialco

Programming: Rich Mercurio

Additional Keyboards/Synthesizers/Programming: Joe Vulpis and Daniel Lapidus

Bass Guitar: Joe Vulpis

Feelings of the Past (1:04)
Concept, Title, and Music Written by: Tara Fialco

Synthesizer: Tara Fialco

Vocal Humming: Dana Fialco

Acoustic Guitar: Tony Di Lullo

Keyboards/Synthesizers: Joe Vulpis

Additional Synthesizers: Daniel Lapidus

Bass Guitar: Joe Vulpis

A Mixture of Feelings (2:16)
Concept, Title, and Music Written by: Tara Fialco

Piano: Tara Fialco

Narration: Dana Fialco

Keyboards/Synthesizers/Orchestration: Joe Vulpis

TA-DA! (3:10)
Concept and Title by: Sharon Fialco

Music and Lyrics Written by: Dana Fialco

Vocals: Dana Fialco and Matt Castle

Piano/Keyboards/Percussion: Joe Vulpis

Guitars: Tony Di Lullo

Bass Guitar: Dave Keyes

Drums: Larry Steppler

Tenor Saxophone: Mark Fineberg

All Music Copyright: © 2010 Fialco Productions, Inc.

Recorded and Mixed at: AP Music Studios, Edgewater, NJ, Villa Musica Studios, New City, NY, and Val Hala Studios, New York, NY

Additional Recording at: The Pod Recording Studio, New York, NY

Produced and Engineered by: Joe Vulpis

Mixed by: Joe Vulpis and Peter Francovilla at AP Music Studios, NY/NJ

Mastered by: Joe Vulpis and Peter Francovilla at AP Music Studios, NY/NJ, and Times Square Mastering

Musical Underscoring by: Joe Vulpis

Additional Underscoring by: Daniel Lapidus and Tara Fialco

Underscoring Consultants: Dana Fialco and Sharon Fialco

Fashion Design by Sharon Fialco:
Starry's jumping for joy ensemble; Starry's riding in the car ensemble; Mommy's coat; Starry's circus ensemble; Starry's trapeze star ensemble; Mommy's circus skirt; Starry's Tumbling Tots ensemble; Starry's "TA-DA!" blouse; and all Starry's hairstyles and hair ornaments

Our Story

BACKGROUND

My pen took off as if it were writing a story on its own. My thoughts could hardly keep up with it. Tara was now a young adult—a college graduate. What was this need to tell her story and rewind back to her earliest days? Was it the result of all the pent-up emotions I had experienced over the years, or was I channeling this from some creative source propelling me to share our experiences with younger parents and their children first starting out on their journey together—to help smooth out the terrain upon which they will travel?

ST. LOUIS, MISSOURI

Our baby girl entered the world marking the proudest moment in our lives—binding us together with a product of our love, providing us with an adorable companion to share our lives going forward. Where would our paths take us? Little did we know how much our new companion would determine that.

What a child she was! Always on the move and full of enthusiasm. Eyes bright with wonder as she explored her world. Along with great abilities and surprising musical talent, Tara would later present perplexing challenges. Was there a name for this puzzling combination? Not able to get a diagnosis, we were left with a MYSTERY.

We were set on a path that we were forced to carve for ourselves, isolated from others. We became creative in overcoming obstacles, bending and twisting to fit into the constraints of mainstream society, often finding ourselves on its periphery. Sustaining us on our journey were love, determination, and endurance. We were surrounded by beautiful music, guided by the light of HOPE.

There would be many questions without answers as Tara grew up. A diagnosis of high-functioning autism would not come until Tara was 21 years old. It unlocked some of the mysteries while opening up new ones. What was its cause? What could be done to help? These are questions faced by countless people with autistic family members today. With this diagnosis, we were no longer alone. We, together with other families, are now on a path seeking to solve this mystery, raising awareness of the prevalence of this condition, searching for a cure, and demanding social justice for our children.

HONOLULU, HAWAII

When Tara was six years old, the gift arrived that would alter our family's life. Tara's grandparents sent their piano from their home in St. Louis, Missouri, to our new home in Honolulu, Hawaii. Tara took to the piano as if it were a part of her. She memorized the sound of every key and soon taught herself to play any music she heard by ear. She began to compose her own music. Through music, she was able to express her thoughts and emotions and reflections on the world around her. The lyrics to her songs showed that she was philosophically precocious. This music would lift us up above some of the harshness in our lives to a place of joy where we experienced pride and gloried in Tara's ability and marveled at the blessing of her gift.

Tara's passage through the school system became the roughest part of our journey. She attended mainstream classes that were structured for convenience with the goals of standardization and conformity. Was it in the mind-set of society to embrace and encourage diversity? Did schools create socially sensitive environments for children with special needs? Did they accommodate unique ways of learning? Did the curricula provide the outlets that encourage growth and belief in oneself for ALL children? Were there opportunities for ALL children to make contributions to enrich their classroom communities? The answer to these questions was NO.

As a parent, I came to realize that besides the daily courage and effort it takes to deal with one's personal challenges, dealing with society can become the even bigger problem.

Often bewildered by the insensitive reaction of other children and her consequential isolation, Tara would come home to her beloved piano (the voice of her soul) and play songs of hope that reflected her belief in the potential goodness in all people. She created a musical, magical world where "all people got along and were accepted exactly the way they were." One of these songs, "Welcome to a Bright New World," became the inspiration for the Starabella series. It is in her music that Tara's generous nature lies. She shares her vision of a better world to include all people.

Dana's arrival into our family three years after Tara's brought the sunshine into our lives. Perhaps other people's days started with the rising sun, but my days did not begin until I kissed Dana good morning and she smiled her dimpled, sunny smile. I took her happy demeanor to be a reflection showing me that as far as she was concerned, I was OK. I gloried in that. Her contentment built my confidence, and we bonded quickly and easily.

Because of Dana's personality, abilities, and talent, our family's path branched off into many interesting directions. We attended school assemblies to see her honored with awards, attended chorus recitals where she was among the soloists, attended plays where she usually had the lead. By sixth grade, she had applied to and was accepted to Punahou School, a prestigious private school in Honolulu. She attended Punahou through high school. She went on to graduate from Brown University.

One person's plight in a family affects every member of that family. Dana took an early interest in Tara's circumstances and her music. Dana began writing lyrics to Tara's music, and they would later perform extensively together throughout our local community. Before one of these performances, Dana introduced Tara this way:

> "Tara has a story to tell. She tells of her experience and feelings growing up with learning differences and her struggle to understand and conform to the world around her and, ultimately, have that world enter hers to discover empathy and understanding together. Tara tells that story beautifully through inspired and inspirational music—a style all her own. She strives with her music to give people courage to reach for their dreams."

Tara's and Dana's paths intersected frequently through their music. They became connected by their musical talent and shared ideals.

We reached a joyful part of our journey when Dana and Tara made their professional debut at the ages of 11 and 14, respectively. They were hired to perform their original compositions, popular music, and Japanese songs at a shopping-center stage on weekends for the next year and a half. It was when she was performing that Tara appeared to glow with a light emanating from within. Dana was in her element, loving to perform. It was during these performances that our family was lifted to a level of joy, by the magic of music, above our daily concerns.

In 1993, Tara and Dana made their first recording of a song called "A New Beginning." Tara had composed "A New Beginning" at age 13, and Dana added the lyrics three years later when she turned 13. The song epitomizes Tara and Dana's joint musical philosophy. When they recorded the song, they hoped to remind people that it is possible and necessary not only to reach each other, but also to gain a greater sense of personal fulfillment and self-realization. They wanted to inspire their listeners to make new beginnings personally, nationally, and globally. These sentiments are just as meaningful today. Dana has recently recorded "A New Beginning" for re-release.

We would reap many rewards along our path when determination paid off. With her innate strength and determination, Tara went on to earn a certificate in Early Childhood Education from Honolulu Community College. She put her education to good use by bringing her musical message to children.

I had been Tara's study buddy. Based on what we learned about child development, I became inspired to write interactive, educational shows for children incorporating Tara's music. Together, Tara and I made props and scenery that we loaded in our station wagon along with her guitar, keyboard, and amplifier. We were "On Our Way"![1] Tara performed these shows solo, occasionally joined by Dana when she was visiting home on college breaks. Tara performed regularly in preschools, kindergarten classrooms, multiple-handicapped elementary school classrooms, day programs, after-school programs, and an intermediate special needs classroom.

[1] In reference to the instrumental "I'm on My Way."

Book Three of Starabella emerged from our observations of children at play at the schools where Tara performed. I noticed that anyone can become the object of ostracism. Combining Tara's childhood dilemmas with those of other children, the story covers a broad spectrum of social situations children confront at school every day. Some of the comments made by Starabella's classmates are the actual words of these children. In 1994, we recorded a version of the Starabella story that incorporated these observations. This version now comprises part of the current Book Three, *Starabella: Welcome to a Bright New World*.

NEW YORK, NEW YORK

Our family made its own "New Beginning" by moving to the thriving island of Manhattan. Here were occupational and artistic opportunities. Plus, there was a network of support for Tara that was unavailable in Honolulu. Tara and Dana performed extensively in many special needs venues in their first years in New York. They are now on separate career paths but still collaborate on recording projects involving their music.

Through the combined efforts of the many parents journeying on their paths, advocating for their children, there are now better educational options for children with special needs. Parents must seek out which program best serves the needs of their individual child. For parents who feel that it compromises their children's civil rights and optimal social and learning potential to be segregated into separate classrooms, more and more children are now members of inclusive classrooms.

When these programs are structured properly to meet the various needs of individual students, all children benefit. Being a member of a diverse learning environment prepares children to feel comfortable in our multicultural, diverse world. Through the Starabella stories, we hope to encourage this trend.

Children who listen to and view Books One and Two celebrate Starabella's accomplishments, feel compassion for her extra challenges, root for her to reach her goals, and gain understanding of her emotions through her music. In this way, they acquire empathy for her by the time she enters kindergarten.

In Book One, children meet Starabella and follow her through babyhood and her early toddler years in the private world of her home. She is the focus of the attention of her family, and they do all they can to meet her needs.

In Book Two, children follow Starabella as she ventures into the community, where there are demands for conformity and expectations for appropriate behaviors and following the rules. She has the supervision, support, and guidance of her parents.

In Book Three, Starabella enters the public arena of kindergarten, where children begin to make their own behavior choices and form their own rules. It is important that they have the guidance in these formative years of caring teachers like Miss Maradise to help them make rules that serve the needs of the whole. This provides firsthand experience in being responsible members of a democratic community.

Starabella and her classmates model the behavior of children who embrace diversity in their friendships and make empathetic social choices. They all work cooperatively to achieve their mutual goal of getting to a "Bright New World."

The journey of producing the Starabella books and recordings serves as a perfect example of the benefits of inclusion. Only through the diverse, creative talents and expertise of each contributor could Starabella and Company come to life.

To quote Mrs. Oclaif, "We are a lucky family," in that we had the opportunity to participate together to produce the Starabella series. Although the inspiration for writing this story stemmed from serious issues and the desire to inspire empathy in children toward one another and provide the tools for change, its actual development brought Tara, Dana, my husband Marvin, and me much joy. We hope children everywhere will see how brilliantly their eyes will shine and how they become empowered when they have the courage to act on their own to reach out a hand to another child … and see that child reach out to another child and on and on and on. These are the hands that can unite the world. "It is only up to you."[2]

---

[2] Lyrics from "I Can Do What I Want to Do."

Contributors

As contributors to the Starabella series, we have all come to the place where our paths meet in HARMONY.

Tara Fialco

Tara's musical compositions provided the seed from which everyone else's creativity grew. It took courage for Tara to revisit the experiences of her childhood so that other children who feel they are on the periphery of the circle of social acceptance will know they are not alone. She wants them to have the courage to keep their dreams alive and for all children to work together to create a world where everyone gets along.

Tara composed the music and wrote many of the lyrics for the musical numbers presented from Starabella's point of view—17 in all. She played the piano and keyboard for all of these songs. Many of the underscoring lines were also taken from tracks of her performances.

Dana Alexandra Fialco

Dana has been singing, performing, and writing her entire life. Her official acting debut came when she was selected to play the starring role in her first-grade play as a caterpillar who turned into a butterfly; she's had the "bug" ever since. She has most recently turned her attention to creating and performing original works.

Dana facilitated many aspects of this production. She collaborated with Joe Vulpis, our music producer, on much of the underscoring and background harmonies for the songs. She also provided me with invaluable feedback on the scripts.

Dana's talents are multifaceted, and her performance on the Starabella CDs sparkles. As the stories' narrator, she created distinctly unique personalities and voices for 13 characters. She composed and wrote the music and lyrics for four original songs, one performed by the teacher and three performed by the parents. The tenderness of her performance reflects her empathy for the characters.

Sharon Fialco

I directed this project, wrote the scripts, and together with my husband, Marvin, published the Starabella series. Marvin and I have been privileged to have our lives filled with the beautiful music of our two wonderful daughters. Much of our family's journey is reflected in this music. I enjoyed providing the words that tied these musical stories together. I also had the opportunity to try my hand at some lyric writing. As an extra bonus, I had fun applying my hobby as a clothes designer to create much of the wardrobe for the stories' characters.

Producing this project has enhanced my life with special meaning and purpose.

J. Marvin Fialco

Marvin is a graduate of the Harvard Business School and Brown University. He was president of Hawaiian King Candies in Honolulu, HI, for 30 years. Marvin's belief in us and in the value of this project for individuals and society as a whole provided Tara, Dana, and me the confidence to persevere in turning our family's dream into reality. He counseled us and we relied on his feedback every step of the way. Without his practical and emotional support, this project would not have been possible.

Gia Williams

Gia is an actress, cabaret artist, and TV hostess. She has toured nationally with the Harlem Gospel Choir and internationally with the Harlem Gospel Ensemble. Her warmth and friendly enthusiasm shine through her stellar performance of Miss Maradise, Starabella's kindergarten teacher.

Matt Castle

Matt Castle is a versatile actor and musician who has appeared in plays, operas, and musical productions across the United States. In 2006, he made his Broadway debut playing Peter in the